O'TOOLE'S ORCHARD

O'TOOLE'S ORCHARD

CHANDLER MCEWAN

O'Toole's Orchard
Copyright © 2010
Chandler McEwan

Cover art & illustrations by Mike Motz Illustrations

ISBN number: 978-0-615-38397-2

FOR INFORMATION CONTACT:

Chandler McEwan

5315 Paris Pike

Georgetown, Ky 40324

859-494-9009

This book is dedicated to my parents,
David and Alice McEwan.

When I think of my father, words like respect, strength,
responsibility, and steadfastness come to mind, so I always
thank him for showing me how to live life.

When I think of my mother, words like grace, benevolence,
lightheartedness, and zest come to mind, so I always thank her
for showing me how to love life as well.

PART ONE

Digger McGillicutty slapped the snooze button on his alarm clock. It was five-thirty. His mind was thick with sleep, but he had to get up. Today represented Digger's only chance to see the gnome, Patrick O'Toole. His grandfather had told him that he must go to O'Toole's Orchard on the St. Patrick's Day following his twelfth birthday. Fear crept into Digger's slumber. What if the German Shepherds trapped him between the wrought iron fence and the stone wall? They would tear him apart. Or what if Michael O'Toole caught Digger in his orchard? He was the most intimidating man that Digger had ever known. His thick black eyebrows. His angry stare. He didn't like kids. He didn't like anybody. Digger couldn't face him. But he had to get up. He had to go today.

Digger's alarm jolted him awake a second time. It was five-forty. What was he doing? He had already lost ten minutes! He sprang from his bed and jerked off his pajamas. On went his shirt, socks, jeans, tennis shoes, jacket and ball cap. He grabbed the coin-sized emerald charm from the table beside his bed and jammed it into his pocket.

Tip-toe

Tip-Toe

Tip-toe

Tip-toe

Tip-toe down the steps and into the kitchen. He spun open the lazy susan cabinet and snatched the brown paper bag that he had packed for his lunch the night before and jammed it into his jacket pocket. He gently unlocked the back door and slipped outside into the pre-dawn darkness. He bounded the back steps in a single leap and immediately hit full stride headed towards O'Toole's Orchard.

He ran up to the corner and turned onto Miller Street. He cut through the alley behind the hospital and then through the playground of the old one-room kindergarten. O'Toole's Orchard was almost a mile from his house and oversleeping meant that Digger had to keep moving fast.

"Six in the morning and six in the evening," his grandfather had said. "That's when that old codger Michael O'Toole calls his dogs with a silent whistle to feed them. And that's the only time that you can get past them and into his orchard."

Digger angled onto Pike Street and pushed himself hard against the steeply sloped road. He listened anxiously for the church bells to begin to chime and hoped that they wouldn't start before he could get to O'Toole's Orchard on the outskirts of town. The orchard was still several hundred yards away.

Digger crossed over the intersection at Elmarch Avenue where the terrain flattened for a bit and he could make better time. He ducked behind a tree to keep from being spotted by an on-coming police car without really knowing why he should hide. The cruiser slowed but didn't stop, and Digger took off again.

He crossed to the other side of Pike Street but once again had to travel uphill. His legs burned and he felt short of breath, but he was getting close to the orchard. He kept running. In the distance, he could hear the German Shepherds began to bark at the sound of his footfalls. Digger shuddered at the thought of the dogs. It seemed almost unthinkable that he planned to trespass on the territory they patrolled between the wrought iron fence and the seven foot stone wall that stood several yards inside the fence. But there was no other way to get into O'Toole's Orchard. The fence and the wall surrounded the entire ten acre estate.

Finally Digger arrived and from the second that he set foot on the sidewalk adjacent to O'Toole's Orchard, the German Shepherds greeted him with the expected animosity. Leaping, growling, barking, sprinting, they stalked his every step and took turns poking their snarling jaws through the pickets in the wrought iron fence. Digger hustled forward cautiously on the far edge of the sidewalk and looked across the street to see if any of the neighbors were reacting to the disturbance. Thankfully, no lights came on.

Digger continued along the sidewalk until he got to his entry point. A bow near the top of one of the pickets of the wrought iron fence would be his gateway. If he grabbed the horizontal top bar and hoisted himself up, he could slither through the opening. Michael O'Toole's home lay around the corner so it was unlikely that the property owner would detect him. He just had to call his dogs at six o'clock as Digger's grandfather had predicted.

Digger squatted down beside a car to catch his breath and keep out of sight. Savage canine yelps pierced his ears. Digger peeked over the car hood to again see if the racket was drawing attention, but he only noticed a single light shining from the backside of a house farther up the road. Digger pulled the emerald charm from his pocket and scooted around to the front of the car so he could see it under the light from the street lamp.

About the size of a silver dollar, the charm had the words of a rhyme inscribed on one side and the gnome's image raised on the other. Were his round friendly face not turned to the beholder, the picture would have been a profile of a man walking in full stride while flipping a coin. Tubby in the middle, Patrick O'Toole was dressed to the hilt with hat, coat, vest, knickers, and long socks that emphasized his disproportionately skinny legs. His shoes looked like elf slippers, long and with a noticeable curlicue at the end.

"Patrick O'Toole will flip the charm up over his head with his right hand and catch it behind his back with his left hand when he's about to do something special," Digger's grandfather had related gleefully. "You never know what to expect from that little gnome, but whatever he does usually comes to some good. He has a knack for helping you along in life. You'll see!"

Digger stood up, walked away from the car, and flipped the charm up over his head with his right hand and tried to catch it behind his back with his left hand. The charm rattled in the gutter. He tried again. The charm hit the gutter again. Digger flipped the charm once more, but this time he caught it. Or, at least, he partially caught it between his hand and his sleeve.

"Maybe that'll bring me some good luck," surmised Digger.

Suddenly, out of nowhere, an ominous intuition advised Digger that he was about to be hammered by something in the road. Instinctively, he started to dart away only to be jerked back roughly.

Digger turned and looked into the face of Bruiser Burnside. Down went the kickstand and off of his bicycle came Bruiser Burnside, still maintaining his firm grip on Digger's collar. As if the dogs weren't enough, now Digger had to deal with Bruiser who was on his morning paper route. Digger was half his size, twice as wise, and unfortunately a person whom Bruiser chose to despise.

"Let me go, Bruiser!" ordered Digger.

And Bruiser did just that. With a heavy handed thrust he sent Digger sprawling toward the fence. Digger landed hard on his hip and one of the German Shepherds nipped him on the hand deep enough to draw blood.

"God, Bruiser! Ya' trying to kill me?" screamed Digger as he scrambled to his feet. Luckily he wasn't bleeding badly. He sucked the blood from the wound. "Jerk!"

"Ya' really made me look stupid yesterday in front of the whole class, didn't ya', ya' little twerp," berated Bruiser, who stood defiantly with his hands on his hips just inviting retaliation.

"I had to answer her, Bruiser. I didn't raise my hand, she just called on me."

"I told you to miss it."

"I can't miss every question, Bruiser."

Bruiser tapped his finger on Digger's chest.

"You better start listening to me, punk, or you are gonna wish you had."

But young Digger wasn't listening to Bruiser even at that moment. On the contrary, he heard the church bells beginning to ring. The dogs' barking began to subside.

They were being called to breakfast! Digger took a quick glance back and could see the dogs departing.

"Cops!" shouted Digger as he pointed down the road.

Bruiser took the bait and the split second that he turned his head to see the imaginary officers of the law, Digger darted forward and pushed him with all his might. Bruiser tumbled back over his bike and crashed into a tangled mess in the gutter.

"Doggone you, Digger McGillicutty!," roared Bruiser. "You're dead meat now!"

Digger turned and leaped, clutching onto the horizontal bar of the fence. Quickly and awkwardly, he contorted his trunk through the bow. Bruiser bounded to his feet and lunged to latch onto Digger's leg, but Digger simultaneously lost his grip on the upper bar and fell with a thud to the ground inside the fence. Bruiser couldn't hold him and Digger jerked his foot out of the bully's reach.

"Come here, ya' common little brat!"

Bruiser grabbed the bars of the fence and with a Herculean effort and a scream of frustration; he tried to pry them farther apart. They didn't budge.

"Dead meat, Digger McGillicutty! Dead meat!"

The commotion alerted the German Shepherds, and a couple of them turned and began charging back toward Digger. Digger panicked. He ran to the wall and leaped but fell back.

"Rip him apart!" rooted Bruiser. "Rip him apart!"

Digger saw a stone that protruded from the wall and instantly leveraged on it to get his arm over the top of the wall. A split second before the dogs arrived, he wrested himself up over the wall.

"Ohhhh," cried out Digger as he crashed down hard on the other side of the wall.

"Dead meat, Digger! Dead meat!" bellowed Bruiser again.

Fortunately, the dogs turned their attention to Bruiser.

"Shut up, you mutts," he scoffed. "I ain't scared of you."

Digger sat silently in the dark at the base of the wall inside O'Toole's Orchard. He almost felt sick from the narrowness of his escape. Fortunately, a few moments later, the dogs barking and Bruiser's ranting began to fade into the distance.

"I'm gonna tell old man O'Toole that you're in his Orchard when I deliver his paper," was the last warning that Bruiser cast in Digger's direction. But Digger knew that threat lacked validity. Bruiser feared Michael O'Toole just as much as Digger did.

Digger noticed a tree nearby and climbed up into it. To this point, his morning had been worse than he had ever imagined. He wanted to feel safe. He pulled himself onto a good solid limb near the trunk and straddled it. He wondered if Michael O'Toole would find him. He wondered if there were more dogs inside the Orchard. He wondered if he might encounter something else that he hadn't anticipated. Most of all, he wondered if he should even have come to O'Toole's Orchard.

.   .   .   .

Digger sat in the tree for a long time. Things seemed calm. He heard only the sound of an occasional car on the road. Gradually, the sun slowly inched up over the eastern horizon, and as it did, Digger's anxieties began to evaporate with the early morning dew. There was no sign of Michael O'Toole. There was no sign of any dogs.

There was no sign of anything unexpected. Instead, he witnessed for the first time the magnificent and mysterious O'Toole's Orchard.

The raw beauty of the Orchard struck Digger immediately. He had never seen a place so inviting. Right in front of him a huge flower garden burst with all the colors of the rainbow. Small white wooden bridges intermittently spanned a stream that dissected the garden and beyond he could see a multitude of ivory-barked birch trees, oak trees, evergreens, and pink dogwoods embellishing the landscape. Lush green grass filled all the open venues and quite a few large stones were scatted strategically throughout the tract. From his spot in the tree that he occupied, he could see a shimmering crystal blue lake about the length of a football field gracing the center of the orchard. A well-maintained dirt pathway appeared to encompass the entire lake.

A brisk, spring breeze suddenly swept through the orchard rustling the leaves on the trees and pushing invisible brooms across random patches of grass. The red and yellow tulips in the garden gently danced in the disturbance.

"My goodness," gasped Digger. "It's like a fairly land."

And it's in bloom! Digger glanced outside the orchard to confirm that the trees outside the orchard were just budding at best.

It can't be. It makes no sense. How could O'Toole's Orchard be in bloom when nothing else was? Digger double checked his discovery. The contrast simultaneously intrigued and puzzled him.

"I gotta check this out," he murmured.

Digger started to climb down from the tree, but before he could really get moving, a small yellow finch landed on the far end of his tree limb. The finch twittered and hopped closer. Digger looked up into the tree to see if he was trespassing in the tree where the bird nested, but saw no sign of its home. The bird hopped closer yet again.

"Come here, little fella," whispered Digger softly as he held out his index finger for the little bird to light upon.

The finch cocked his head as if considering whether or not to accept the invitation. Then it flew off and landed on one of the small white bridges nearby. It hopped up and down and twittered loudly, while appearing to be looking at Digger the whole time.

Digger thought this was very odd but didn't move.

The finch came right back and landed on the limb again.

"What do you want, little bird," laughed Digger, who was more curious than ever.

The yellow finch then flew up in the air and startlingly close to Digger's face before sailing back over to the same wooden bridge.

Digger didn't really believe what was happening, but he felt compelled to follow. He dropped down out of the tree and headed towards the bird on the bridge. The myriad of fears that had haunted Digger earlier were now completely gone. If anything, he felt a mystifying sense of security. The orchard seemed so peaceful and enticing. He glided along effortlessly as if in some sort of dream or reverie. The sun brightened his outlook. The pleasantly cool air refreshed him. A smattering of puffy white clouds drifted lazily across the sky. And best of all, Digger had this exquisite place all to himself.

When Digger got close to the bridge, the little finch flew off once again and landed on a limb of a massive oak tree near the lake. The oak tree had a large hole near its base and Digger immediately sprinted towards it.

Digger peered inside the hole.

"Patrick O'Toole," he called hopefully. "Patrick O'Toole."

Digger looked up at the finch perched above him. The little bird twittered once and cocked his head as if instructing Digger to investigate the hole again.

"Patrick O'Toole," he implored more loudly. "The gnome, Patrick O'Toole."

Nothing happened.

Digger stuck his arm inside the tree, but felt nothing. Then he stuck his head inside the tree and saw nothing. Digger stood up and carefully placed one foot inside the tree and then the other. Surprisingly, he stood without touching anything. Darkness enveloped him. He felt forward with his arms like a sleepwalker and took one - two - three - four - five steps inside the tree.

In a flash, Digger hopped back outside the tree and skirted around its trunk to verify its circumference. It was quite impossible that he could walk inside the tree. He climbed back inside the tree and took five - ten – fifteen - twenty steps before instinctively stopping. His mind began racing and wrestling with the totally illogical idea that this tree was somehow wider on the inside than it was on the outside.

As Digger stood there silently pondering, he heard a noise in the distance. It sounded like a twig breaking under the pressure of a footfall. He listened more closely and sensed something moving in his direction. Was it Patrick O'Toole? Was it something else?

Digger hurdled back outside the tree, pulled the charm from his pocket, and dropped it on the worn dirt spot beneath the hole. He scampered across the dirt path as fast as his legs would carry him and dove in behind an evergreen. He nestled himself on his knees in the grass and parted the branches in front of him to get an unobstructed view of the ever-so-strange tree across the way. Then, in a whispering voice, he recited the words of the rhyme on the charm.

"The luck of the Irish

is always at play

In O`Toole's Orchard

on St. Patrick's Day.

PART TWO

With his knees tucked up under his chin, Patrick O'Toole came cannon-balling through the opening in that old oak tree with the startling suddenness of bread popping from a toaster. In a single deft motion, which betrayed his pudgy physique, he scooped up the charm with a swooping right hand before his feet even touched the ground.

"Me Charm!" he rejoiced, giving a little jump for joy. His face beamed with excitement. Then he flipped the charm up over his head, caught it behind his back, and instantly disappeared!

Digger looked left, right, and finally up before spotting the clever gnome sitting cross-legged near the top of his oak tree on a branch that was positively not thick enough to be supporting him. The little yellow finch sailed up from his limb and landed on Patrick's shoulder.

"Look, Mr. Finch," said the gnome as he displayed the charm between his thumb and his index finger. "I found me charm on St. Patrick's Day. What do ya think of that?"

Perhaps thinking that Patrick was trying to feed him, the little bird pecked at the charm and knocked it from the gnome's grasp. Digger started to dash from behind the evergreen to ensure that the emerald charm didn't get lost in the grass, but, to his astonishment, Patrick O'Toole was somehow already waiting on the ground to catch the charm himself.

How on earth did he get down there so fast, wondered Digger? Nobody can move that quickly.

The gnome stuffed the charm in his pocket and walked back over to the hole in his old oak tree and dropped to his knees. He reached inside the hole and began to search for something. He banged and clanged through what sounded like a toolbox before coming away with a silver mug, a mallet and a spike. The spike was huge, no less than a foot long with a head the size of a man's fist.

The gnome walked over to the tree adjacent to his and, bending down, tapped the spike gently to give it a start into the bark. Then, looking very much like a little boy playing baseball, he drew back the mallet about waist level, cocked up his front leg, and miraculously drove the spike completely into the tree on the first blow.

"Don't mind if I do," he said.

Then Patrick pulled open the head of the spike and drew a golden liquid from the tree. A thick, white foam formed at the top of his mug.

He raised the mug to eye level but an arm's length away.

"A toast to St. Patrick's Day," he proposed. His Irish accent was faithful, and so was his Irish taste. The gnome drank that entire brew and drew another.

Digger grew more comfortable with each passing moment and was on the verge of having enough courage to reveal himself to the gnome when he detected the most gentle of sensations on his leg. Incredibly, he discovered a chipmunk, standing with its hind legs on the ground and its two tiny front feet resting upon Digger's knee. The chipmunk sniffed the air and stared directly at Digger's face. Both amused and charmed, Digger grinned at the precious little rodent while touching his finger to his lips to signal quiet.

The miniature creature had other ideas, however, and scampered away from Digger and right over to Patrick O'Toole. It reached up and grabbed the curlicue of the gnome's shoe and began tugging ferociously.

"Well good morning, me little friend," acknowledged Patrick. "Are ya wantin' to lick the bottom of me mug when I'm finished?"

The chipmunk ignored the offer and began squeaking loudly and pointing towards the evergreen where Digger was hiding.

"Well now," mused Patrick more seriously. "Have ya noticed somethin' a bit strange in me orchard?"

Delighted at being understood, the chipmunk jumped up and down and squealed in a clamorous confirmation. Patrick O'Toole calmly took another sip of his beverage, then vanished yet again!

Digger looked up, down, left, and right, but Patrick O'Toole was nowhere in sight. Digger rose from his knees to expand the scope of his vision, but still didn't see the gnome anywhere. A few seconds later, Digger felt a finger gently tapping on his shoulder. Oh my goodness, thought Digger without even turning to look. I came looking for Patrick O'Toole and now he's found me.

.   .   .   .

Based on what his grandfather had told him about Patrick O'Toole, Digger could not have imagined the little gnome to be anything other than a gentle and jovial character and he wasn't disappointed. From the moment of their first encounter, the gnome's words and body language conveyed to Digger that his presence in the orchard was not only welcome, but very much desired. Patrick's genuine smile, twinkling green eyes, and gracious disposition put Digger at ease right away. Moreover, the gnome actually stood a few inches shorter than Digger and behaved so playfully that Digger felt like he had happened upon a wonderful new friend rather than an authority figure.

Spending time with Patrick O'Toole proved to be an exceptional experience right from the start. Good cheer and unique ideas flowed freely from the little fellow. In fact, at one point in the morning, the imaginative gnome somehow had the finch and the chipmunk engaged in a game whereupon the small yellow bird would drop a leaf from a tree and the chipmunk would try to catch it before it hit the ground.   As the chipmunk darted, stopped, and dashed yet again trying to position itself beneath the wistfully whirling foliage, the animated little gnome concurrently moved and contorted his body and shouted encouragement and instructions to his tiny friend.   When the exhausted chipmunk finally caught a leaf on the fourth or fifth try, Patrick pumped his fist and danced around his tree as if his homeland had won a World Cup Soccer match.

The morning's activities included baseball as well. When Digger mentioned that he enjoyed the game, the little gnome promptly produced a ball and two gloves from his oak tree. Patrick tossed Digger the catcher's mitt and found a stick to be the mound and a flat stone to be the plate.   Each of Patrick's pitches was preceded by an elaborate wind-up and succeeded by the gnome's announcement of "Ball one!" or "Strike Two!" or whatever was appropriate.   Not surprisingly, Patrick had a conveniently liberal strike zone. If Digger didn't have to leap or lunge to catch the ball, the little gnome boisterously declared his throw a strike.

The two skipped stones on the lake. They played a game of badminton. They even invented a game of football against imaginary opponents with Patrick O'Toole assuming the role of quarterback and Digger pretending to be the receiver. Finally, both the little gnome and Digger admitted to being a little tired and hungry. Since it was about noon, they decided to take a much needed lunch break under one of the orchard's many sprawling trees. Digger started in on his sandwich and cookies while Patrick drew another mug of refreshment.

"Aye, lad, ya've worn me out," confessed Patrick. "How about we just take a little stroll around me orchard after lunch?"

"Okay," replied Digger most willingly.

Anything the little gnome suggested was fine with Digger.

.   .   .   .

After their short rest, Digger and Patrick O'Toole began their walk. The pair had journeyed about halfway around the lake when they came upon a stone vault that was built into the side of a knoll. The dirt path split into two walkways encircling the mound. A heavy looking metal door with a small barred window held the dead in their chamber, and, as they drew closer, the inscriptions in the stone above the entrance caught Digger's eye. Apparently, the tomb held three prisoners of the past.

Clarence	Sylvester	William Jennings
Darrow	Court Jester	Bryan
R.I.P.	R.I.P.	R.I.P.

Digger stopped short of the tomb, and found it curious that Patrick walked right up to the front door of the vault as if he were approaching the home of a close acquaintance.

"What are you doing, Mr. O'Toole?" inquired Digger.

"I just thought ya might take a minute to meet a few friends of mine," responded Patrick O'Toole.

Digger guessed that the little gnome had planned some sort of practical joke. He decided to play along and re-read the inscriptions.

"I suppose you mean Clarence Darrow, William Jennings Bryan, and Sylvester, the Court Jester?" obliged Digger.

"That's right," confirmed Patrick.

"Ha!" cackled Digger loudly. "I'm not that dumb, Mr. O'Toole. It says R.I.P. - rest in peace. Those guys are dead!"

Patrick O'Toole glanced at the inscriptions and shuffled his feet.

"No, no, no, they're not dead," he refuted. "Besides, I've always heard that R.I.P. stands for ... 'right inside . . . probably'."

Digger burst into laughter.

"You're crazy, Patrick O'Toole," he exclaimed cheerfully. Energized by the little gnome's frivolity, Digger sprinted around to the grassy backside of the knoll and climbed up so that he could position himself on top of the vault.

Then it happened again! At the very moment that Digger completed his ascent to his lofty perch, he saw the little gnome give his coin a toss. Spinning heads over tails, the charm popped from his right hand and sailed neatly over his head only to be snatched ever-so-cleverly by his left hand waiting behind his back. And no sooner had he caught his charm than the little gnome gave a close-fisted rap-rap-rap on the metal door of the vault.

Before Digger had a chance to ridicule Patrick's nonsensical knock, he was rendered steadfastly dumbfounded by what happened next. For not only did the vault's door boldly swing open, but even more shockingly, a jester on a unicycle instantaneously emerged.

It would have been evident to the dullest of minds, and Digger certainly knew straightaway, that this man was Sylvester, the Court Jester. He wore what looked like a yellow, silken bodysuit with flared blue trim around his waist and shoulders. Aboard his head was a nightcap with long rabbit ears that were broken in the middle by the weight of the small golden jingle bells on their ends. Multicolored rings decorated his wrists and ankles and long pointed shoes donned his feet. He appeared to be a thin man, but had the round youthful face of a child.

Digger quickly scurried back down from the top of the vault and hopped on a stone to be part of the action. He immediately concluded that this jester was an unusual and charming character. He rode about Patrick and Digger on his unicycle in unpredictable circles and figure-eights but spoke not a word. He teetered and tottered and teased that he might tumble, only to make nifty recoveries that proved he was never out of control in the first place. He smiled as he cycled like a child at play, and could, when he chose, cycle in place. He made purposeful maneuvers, apparently for balance, with a wand-like object that he held in his hand.

Finally, the jester acknowledged Patrick with a nod of his head and rode over and stopped in front of Digger.

"And you must be Digger McGillicutty," he deduced in a crisp but pleasant voice.

"Yes, sir," replied Digger, wondering how the court jester knew his name.

"The Guest of Honor has arrived!" announced Sylvester joyfully. "Mr. Bryan and Mr. Darrow will be so pleased. They've been anxiously awaiting your arrival."

"They have?" responded the bewildered child.

"Indeed, they have," declared Sylvester who reached out with his wand and gently pushed the bill of Digger's baseball cap down over his eyes. "And do you know where Mr. Bryan and Mr. Darrow are now, Digger?"

"No!?!" retorted Digger as he straightened his cap and slid off the stone. He didn't know why he was the guest of honor; he had no way of knowing where the two gentlemen were; and, he absolutely didn't appreciate being asked that question by someone who had just pushed the bill of his cap down over his eyes.

The jester just smiled coyly at Digger and backpedaled over to the door of the vault. He tapped his wand gently against the epitaph.

"Well, they're . . . right inside . . . probably," he chided impishly.

Having validated Patrick O'Toole's less conventional interpretation of the graveyard acronym, Sylvester went back inside the vault, but his absence lasted only a few seconds. For no sooner had he disappeared than he re-appeared leading two well-dressed men who were pushing a cart which carried a large sheet-covered object. Visibly straining, the short stocky man and the tall slender man lifted the object off the cart and set it on the ground. Then Sylvester laid his wand upon the sheet.

"Voila!"

And with his wand, the jester drew the covering from the object revealing a marvelously noble piece of woodwork. This podium had curves and swirls and clearly had been made from the finest timber. Most noticeably, on the front of the podium was a fairly large and splendidly carved picture of a boy with a baseball cap. In disbelief, Digger drew closer only to confirm that the picture unmistakably resembled none other than himself. Completely perplexed, Digger had no idea what to do or say.

The short man and the tall man made a trip back into the vault, and like Sylvester, they returned posthaste. Oddly, the short man came out carrying an exceptionally tall chair which appeared to have been made from a tree stump. The tall man returned carrying a demonstratively shorter chair. The short man positioned the tree-stump as a seat for the occupant of the podium. The tall man stationed the more normal chair opposite the podium about ten feet away.

Digger gravitated towards the tree stump and discovered that, although its seat was nearly up to his shoulders, it was just the right height for anyone who might be sitting at the podium.

"OK!" commanded Patrick O'Toole. "Everyone take their places."

With the exception of Digger, everyone else seemed to know exactly where to go.

"Wait a minute. I don't get it," lamented Digger. "I don't know what we're doing or where I'm supposed to go."

The court jester rode over to Digger and again pushed down the bill of his cap with his wand.

"Don't you see?" teased Sylvester.

"No!?!" shot back Digger.

But actually, it was obvious. Patrick O'Toole had taken his place a few feet to the left of the podium and Sylvester cycled over and stopped a few feet from the right. The two men stood on either side of the small chair

across from the podium, all of which forced Digger to conclude that the tree stump behind the stand with his picture on it must certainly be his place.

"I still don't get it," he protested as he literally climbed onto the stump. "What are we doing?"

Patrick O'Toole then proceeded to explain to Digger that the short heavy-set man, William Jennings Bryan, and the tall man with the pony tail, Clarence Darrow, had been having a dispute for years. William Jennings Bryan had been arguing the merits of religion while Clarence Darrow had been defending the science of evolution. The disagreement had been so long-running that both men had agreed that they needed a third person to settle their debate.

"But then," interjected Mr. Bryan. "Mr. Darrow and I couldn't agree on the third party, or arbitrator, as I like to call it."

"Until I suggested that we let the next person who comes along be the arbitrator," chimed in Mr. Darrow.

"And since we didn't know who the next person to come along might be, it was clear that we would have an arbitrary arbitrator," explained Mr. Bryan.

"An arbitrary arbitrator was agreed indeed," confirmed Mr. Darrow.

Digger didn't need any help figuring out that he had been selected as the arbitrary arbitrator. Furthermore, the idea intimidated him and he reacted by immediately trying to relieve himself of the responsibility. First, he suggested that Patrick O'Toole would be more qualified for the duty, but Mr. Darrow pointed out that the gnome had already been considered and rejected prior to the decision to have an arbitrary arbitrator. So Digger nominated Sylvester, but both Mr. Bryan and Mr. Darrow emphatically discarded that suggestion as unacceptable.

"Just a clown on a unicycle," pointed out Mr. Darrow.

"Besides," added Mr. Bryan, "Sylvester's been staying with us for quite a while and does not fit the standard of the next person to come along."

"That's absolutely right!" agreed Mr. Darrow. "It can't be Sylvester."

"But I'm just a kid," protested Digger. "I'm just twelve years old. I don't have any idea who's right or wrong."

"Splendid!" exclaimed Mr. Bryan. "An open-minded arbitrary arbitrator is just what we need."

"It's more than we could have hoped for," concurred Mr. Darrow.

"The lad will be a perfect arbitrary arbitrator," chimed in Sylvester, who pedaled over to Digger, performed a meaningless pirouette, and pulled from his pocket a wooden gavel, which he laid on the podium.

"You'll do fine."

"I don't think so," objected Digger. "I've got no business being the judge"

Digger glanced at Patrick hoping to get some last second support, but the little gnome instead offered a vote of confidence with a wink and a nod. At that point, Digger knew that he wasn't going to escape this obligation. His grandfather had assured him that he could trust Patrick O'Toole so Digger just concluded that maybe the gnome had another trick up his sleeve.

Digger picked up the gavel, hesitated for a moment, then begrudgingly pounded the podium to call the court to order.

.   .   .   .

Mr. Bryan and Mr. Darrow went quickly about their business and determined that each would take a turn in the witness chair at the expense of the other's questioning. After both men had the opportunity to defend their cause, Digger would render his decision based on which argument stood strongest against the opponent's challenges. The two men officially designated Patrick O'Toole as sergeant-at-arms and Sylvester as the court jester.

As Patrick O'Toole began the proceedings by swearing in Mr. Darrow, Digger found himself distracted by the merrily traversing court jester. He wheeled and darted, stopped and started, and circled back around to where he departed. Backwards and forwards, fast or slow, there was no way to know just how he might go. Then, just as Mr. Darrow sat down in the witness chair, Sylvester stopped at his spot and riddled the court with a rhyme.

Methinks, methinks, they think too much

They think too much for me.

Some think like this, some think like that

But no one thinks like me.

Mr. Bryan, Mr. Darrow, and Patrick O'Toole paid little or no attention to the jester's rhyme, but the poem certainly intrigued Digger. Even as Mr. Bryan began questioning Mr. Darrow, Digger rolled the words over in his mind. *Methinks, methinks, they think too much. They think too much for me. Some think like this, some think like that, but no one thinks like me.*

Why did Sylvester say that? What did he mean? Digger looked over at the court jester who was staring back at him. Sylvester opened his eyes as wide as possible and rolled his glare over to the two combatants as if instructing Digger to pay attention.

Digger had absorbed enough of the two men's exchange to know that Mr. Bryan had been asking Mr. Darrow about his qualifications and background. He also detected that both men were exceedingly serious about the subject matter and fiercely determined to gain the upper hand. Digger's stomach churned with anxiety.

"Mr. Darrow," asked Mr. Bryan, "could you tell the court who originally came up with this Theory of Evolution?"

"The Theory of Evolution was first presented by Charles Darwin in his famous book entitled <u>The Origin of the Species</u>," responded Mr. Darrow.

"And could you summarize for us, Mr. Darrow, just what this book, <u>The Origin of the Species</u>, says?"

"The book puts forth two basic ideas. First, that only the fittest survive in nature. And secondly, that humans evolved over a long period of time from an ape-like creature."

"So, Mr. Darrow, do you believe that you descended from an ape-like creature?"

"Yes, Mr. Bryan, I believe that all humans did."

"So I guess it's fair to assume, Mr. Darrow, that you are sometimes overcome with an irrepressible urge to live in a tree house and diet on bananas alone?"

Mr. Darrow stared disgustedly at Mr. Bryan while the latter chuckled and shot a self assured glance at Digger.

"No, Mr. Bryan," responded Mr. Darrow sourly. "I have never had such urges."

"Well, I would have thought that someone who believed that he evolved from an ape would at least have experienced some ape-like tendencies," explained Mr. Bryan innocently. "But if not, then could you tell us why you believe that man evolved from the ape?"

"In his book, Charles Darwin explains the process of evolution in great detail but the reason that I accept evolution is because it's a scientific fact that the bone structure of a human being matches exactly the bone structure of an ape."

"That's an impressive finding, Mr. Darrow. But did Mr. Darwin point out any other examples of one specie evolving into another?

"Yes, Mr. Bryan, flying squirrels may well have evolved into bats."

"So evolution is a common process in the natural world. Is that correct?"

"Absolutely."

"Well, then, Mr. Darrow, why don't we see evolution taking place today? I never hear anything about lions evolving into tigers or zebras evolving into horses in this day and age. With all our scientific technology, surely you can give us an example of some specie that is in the process of evolving into another specie right here and now."

"Evolution doesn't happen overnight, Mr. Bryan. It takes millions of years."

"In other words, you can't give me any examples. Can you, Mr. Darrow?" snapped Mr. Bryan, who promptly continued without giving his adversary a chance to respond. "Alright, my good man, could you tell us where the ape came from?"

"Most evolutionists believe that life as we know it began in the seas and gradually made its way onto land, Mr. Bryan."

"And where would these scientists say that the land and seas came from, Mr. Darrow?"

"Most scientists subscribe to the Big Bang theory. That is, they believe that all the matter in the universe exploded from a core of matter and formed the solar systems and galaxies as we know them today."

Mr. Bryan stared at Digger for a moment to assure he had the young man's attention.

"Let me see if I have this right, Mr. Darrow," he began. "Once upon a time there was this ball of matter that suddenly exploded one day and just happened to form into the universe as we know it. And on this one little planet that we call Earth, life began to form in the oceans. Then that life expanded into many different forms and eventually spread to land where the ape evolved into man. Is that what you'd have us believe, Mr. Darrow?"

"I wouldn't have stated it that way, but I'd say that you have the basic idea."

"Well, now," scoffed Mr. Bryan, "I can't speak for everybody, but that theory sounds like quite a tale to me. Maybe a more scientific name for that theory would be the Really Lucky Big Bang. Wouldn't you agree, Mr. Darrow?"

"No," responded Mr. Darrow harshly. "I absolutely would not agree."

From that moment forward, tensions sky-rocketed. Mr. Bryan kept firing questions at Mr. Darrow and Mr.

Darrow kept firing back responses. Heated exchange followed heated exchange. The two men positively got into each other's face. Digger glanced at Patrick O"Toole who smiled and wiped his brow as if he too sensed the venom in the debate.

When Mr. Bryan finally finished questioning Mr. Darrow, Digger had the distinct feeling that Mr. Bryan had gained the upper hand. This result pleased Digger immensely. With a clear-cut winner, he anticipated that his decision at the end of the day would be fairly easy. However, before Digger had time to relax and catch his breath, he found the two adversaries battling anew. This time, Mr. Bryan had taken the chair and Mr. Darrow paced back and forth cross-examining him.

"Mr. Bryan, do you believe the stories in the Bible are symbolic or do you accept them literally?" asked Mr. Darrow.

"I accept the Bible as it is written, Mr. Darrow."

"Then you must believe that the earth was created in a few short days."

"That's right, Mr. Darrow, the entire universe was created in precisely six days. On the seventh day, God rested."

"And as a scholar of the Bible, Mr. Bryan, do you know on which day the sun was created?"

"Yes, Mr. Darrow, the sun was created on the fourth day."

"Then tell me, Mr. Bryan, how did it happen that there was a morning and evening on the first day of creation? Was there a morning and evening without the sun?"

Mr. Bryan squirmed in his seat but did not respond right away.

"Thanks for clearing that up," interjected Mr. Darrow sarcastically. "Now illuminate me on something else, Mr.

Bryan. Do you believe that Adam and Eve are the parents of all human kind?"

"I do."

"Well, if Adam and Eve begat all humans, Mr. Bryan, then how did this planet of ours come to have so many different people and races?"

"If you remember the story of the tower of Babel, Mr. Darrow, then you know that God stopped the people from building a tower to heaven by giving them seven different tongues or languages. The people then scattered to the corners of the earth according to their languages."

"But that didn't change the gene pool, Mr. Bryan. Did God breathe life into some other clay figures that the Bible doesn't tell us about?"

"No, Mr. Darrow, these people grew up in different climates and environments and speaking different languages, so naturally they became very different."

"Do I hear you saying that they evolved, Mr. Bryan?" asked Mr. Darrow as he shot a triumphant wink at Digger.

"They may have evolved, Mr. Darrow," replied Mr. Bryan, "but they certainly didn't evolve from an ape."

The momentum change startled Digger. Maybe this wasn't going to be such an easy decision after all.

"Let me ask you something else," persisted Mr. Darrow. "Do you really believe that Noah built an ark and was able to gather up two of every kind of animal?"

"I do."

"Don't you realize, Mr. Bryan, what an impossible task that would have been? You're talking about thousands of different animals from all the different continents being gathered together in one place at the same time. Do you really believe that one man could do that?"

"Perhaps the rains drove them to high grounds where the Ark was, Mr. Darrow."

"Right, Mr. Bryan, and by some miraculous coincidence, exactly one male and one female of each specie just happened to show up. Then all these animals magically shed their instinct to kill and eat their natural prey, and climbed on the boat in an orderly fashion. Are you saying that really happened?"

"The Bible says it did, Mr. Darrow. That's good enough for me."

Mr. Darrow purposefully paused, looked at Digger, and shook his head incredulously.

"Tell me something else, Mr. Bryan," he continued. "Did all living creatures not contained on the Ark die during the flood?"

"Quite obviously, all living creatures not contained on the Ark drowned during the flood. When you talk about this flood, Mr. Darrow, you're talking about the greatest flood of all time. Forty straight days and forty straight nights of rain."

"But what about the fish, Mr. Bryan, did they drown also?"

Mr. Bryan hesitated again and Mr. Darrow seized the opportunity to attack.

"Yes, Mr. Bryan, what about the fish? Did they live through the flood, or against all probabilities, did they drown? Or maybe Noah had whales and sharks and crabs and jellyfish on the Ark as well - and it just wasn't mentioned?"

Mr. Bryan exhaled heavily.

"The fish may have lived," he conceded.

"The fish may have lived," echoed Mr. Darrow emphatically. "And speaking of fish, Mr. Bryan, do you really believe Jonah lived inside a whale for three days?"

"I believe, Mr. Darrow, in a God who can make a man, make a whale, and make both do what He pleases."

"Adam and Eve didn't do as He pleased."

"Adam and Eve yielded to the temptation of the forbidden fruit from the Tree of Knowledge and the lowly serpent, an agent of the Devil," expounded Mr. Bryan. "Besides, at least Christianity provides an explanation as to why man is the only creature to wear clothes, which is more that I can say for science."

"Oh, you're so right, Mr. Bryan," acknowledged Mr. Darrow mockingly. "Scientists have wasted a lot of time looking for that amazing apple tree and the talking snake."

Blood pressures exploded once again. Like two great swordsmen fencing, first Mr. Bryan had advanced and now Mr. Darrow. Prodding, pushing, thrusting into the mysteries of human history, they debated gallantly for the spoils of victory. Mr. Darrow challenged Mr. Bryan on the accuracy of Moses parting the Red Sea, Daniel in the lion's den, and any other facet of Biblical writings that he deemed vulnerable. Mr. Bryan fought back tirelessly and defiantly.

Finally, mercifully, the confrontation ended. The intensity of the debate had exhausted Digger. To make matters worse, Mr. Bryan had clearly relinquished the edge established while Mr. Darrow was in the witness chair. Digger dreaded the idea of declaring a winner. Unfortunately, the little gnome unwittingly added to the pressure of the moment.

"Okay Digger, ya've heard both sides," noted Patrick within moments after Mr. Darrow finished his questioning. "Give us your verdict."

"Can I have a few minutes to think about it?" asked Digger.

"Why certainly, lad, take your time" responded the gnome graciously. "I didn't mean to rush ya. Take all the time ya need."

Time Digger needed and time Digger took. Fifteen, thirty, forty-five minutes passed. In his mind, Digger wrestled with the strengths and weaknesses of both arguments. The confrontation between Mr. Bryan and Mr. Darrow not only highlighted the virtues that Digger saw in each philosophy, but it also reminded him of the doubts that prevented him from totally embracing either concept as well. Without question, Digger wanted to end this ordeal quickly. But he also wanted to get it right.

An hour passed.

The pressure mounted and weighed heavily on Digger. At one point, he determined that he would just declare Mr. Bryan the winner, but that didn't seem fair to Mr. Darrow. Then he decided that Mr. Darrow had won, but he couldn't make that call either.

Patrick O'Toole grew weary of waiting and took a seat in the witness chair. The two well dressed gentlemen paced and paused and paced again. From time to time, each would check his watch. Digger felt like one or the other was always casting an impatient glance his way. In fact, only Sylvester seemed undisturbed by the delay. He cycled playfully as if he had all the time in the world. He swerved and curved and leaned and streamed around and about all who were present. A happy person was this jester, a completely uninhibited exception to the rule.

Just watching the jester gave Digger a few moments of much needed relief from the task at hand. Secretly, he longed for the same carefree feeling.

Sylvester noticed Digger watching him and forthwith halted his cycling right in front of the young arbitrary arbitrator. Although Digger expected a mild scolding for not adhering to business, the jester instead delighted Digger with a lively repetition of his rhyme.

Methinks, methinks, they think too much

They think too much for me.

Some think like this, some think like that

But no one thinks like me.

Digger laughed. The jester's lighthearted nature captivated him. The clown's catchy rhyme tickled his curiosity.

"So what do you think, Sylvester?" inquired Digger casually.

Sylvester greeted Digger's question with a warm and receptive smile as if to say, "I thought you'd never ask."

"The beauty and harmony of nature leads me to believe that there must be a Creator, Digger," began the jester calmly, "but the world is always changing. Volcanoes erupt. Glaciers melt. Earthquakes rattle the ground beneath our feet and meteors shoot through the

heavens. In far away galaxies stars explode. With the natural world in a constant state of flux, it only makes sense to me that God would have the intelligence to design life so that it could evolve and adapt to its changing environment."

The jester spun and sped away.

"Don't listen to him," instructed Mr. Bryan.

"Just a clown on a unicycle," pointed out Mr. Darrow.

But Digger was listening to the clown on the unicycle. The solar system fascinated Digger and he marveled at how the moon went around the earth and the earth went around the sun and how it all worked so perfectly. Sea turtles instinctively crawling towards the ocean at birth and birds knowing how to build nests in trees mystified Digger as well. Yet, Sylvester was right. Things were always changing. Heck! Digger himself was changing.

The young lad snatched the gavel and pounded the podium.

"Alright," he announced. "I've come to a decision."

Mr. Darrow and Mr. Bryan glanced at each other in curious anticipation and came and stood before their arbitrary arbitrator. Patrick rose to his feet.

"When I look around myself, I see a world that's too magnificent to have just happened. But everything is in motion and always changing too. So like Sylvester said, maybe God had to create life forms that could adapt and evolve," explained Digger. "That makes both Mr. Bryan and Mr. Darrow a little bit right and a little bit wrong. And since Sylvester pointed this out to me, I hereby declare that Sylvester, the Court Jester, is the winner of this debate."

"Preposterous!" protested Mr. Darrow adamantly.

"Out of the question," echoed Mr. Bryan with the same displeasure.

Digger looked to Sylvester for some much needed support, but the court jester zipped right by him and back into the vault. A few moments later, thankfully, his cycling ally returned carrying a second unicycle. He rode right up to Digger.

"Would you like to give it a try?" asked the jester.

Digger looked the unicycle over and recalled his first experience on a bicycle.

"I'd bust my tail," he replied matter-of-factly.

"Oh, I won't let that happen," assured Sylvester.

And the court jester, quite astonishingly, balanced the unicycle on his wand and held it up for Digger to mount from his stump at the podium. The temptation was too much for Digger to resist. Cautiously, Digger boarded the air borne bike as Sylvester whispered instructions.

"Saddle your feet on the pedals. Keep your back upright and your weight on the seat. Arms out for balance. Eyes straight ahead."

Digger began to pedal and get a feel for the unicycle while the jester magically kept him aloft. Gradually, Sylvester lowered him down to the ground. Then, at the very instant that the tire touched the turf, Digger shot forward on a huge and wild loop away from the vault. He barely missed a head-on collision with an oak tree and had to turn sharply to avoid a chilling March dip into the lake. He brushed through the limbs of an evergreen and sent those on foot scattering for safety before beginning to gain control.

"Hey! This is fun!" exclaimed Digger as he circled around the courtroom.

Sylvester took up residence on his own cycle just behind Digger and mimicked the young lad's every swerve and swivel.

"Quit playing around, young man, and give us your real decision," barked Mr. Darrow.

"I already did," countered Digger.

"You can not be serious," growled Mr. Bryan.

Digger whirled and wheeled away from the gentlemen, and as he did, the trailing court jester gently touched his wand to the top of Digger's baseball cap. Suddenly, Digger took on the personality of the jester and rode back to Mr. Bryan and Mr. Darrow to finalize his decision with a rhyme of his own.

Methinks, methinks, no one can prove

Just how we came to be.

I wish I could, but know I can't

Go back in time to see.

Oh what a plight! I got uptight.

The verdict left to me.

Sylvester's rhyme came just in time

With him I do agree!!!

Sylvester and Patrick roared with laughter and approval. Digger cackled loudly. His heart sailed happily and freely as if it were riding on a soft and swiftly moving cloud. Spontaneously, the pair of cyclists began to put on a show. They started weaving and achieving such perfectly timed acrobatic feats that any bystander would have wagered that the two had been partners in an act for years.

Patrick cheered and joined in their merriment, but Messrs. Bryan and Darrow were not nearly as jubilant. Unable to hide their disappointment, the two gentlemen muttered angrily to each other as they began hauling the podium, stump, and chair back into the vault. Disparaging remarks such as 'ridiculous' and 'foolhardy' were hurled in Digger's direction, but the lad was too relieved and elated to acknowledge them. Thankfully for Digger, the opponents soon resorted to blaming one another for the unintended outcome. Shortly thereafter, the last remnant of the courtroom set disappeared from sight for good and Digger neither heard nor saw the disgruntled gentlemen again.

The gnome, the clown, and the boy continued celebrating the occasion as long as they could. Lemonade served as the drink for a toast and all three shared in the fun. Unfortunately however, even good times must come to an end. All too abruptly for Digger came the high-fives, the good-byes, and the sight of the heavy vault door slamming shut behind Sylvester.

Digger hurried over to the door of the vault and latched onto the window bars so that he could hoist himself up to have a look inside, but was distracted by the gnome's voice.

"Race ya back to my tree, Digger McGillicutty," hollered Patrick O'Toole, who was already running ahead and had built up a sizeable lead. "Might be bad if ya lost a race to a little old gnome."

Digger promptly accepted the challenge and took off after the little gnome. Patrick managed to stay in front until Digger sprinted by him about thirty yards from the finish. However, when Digger looked back to verify his advantage, he didn't see his smallish companion behind him.

Digger slowed his pace and kept looking back but didn't see Patrick O'Toole until he got to the gnome's tree and found him sitting comfortably on a large rock by the lake.

"Thought ya'd never get here," taunted the gnome playfully.

Digger pushed Patrick gently on the shoulder.

"I don't know what you did, Patrick," stated Digger. "But you did something to get ahead of me. Flipped your charm or something."

"Now lad, would I do somethin' like that?" laughed Patrick.

"I think you would," replied Digger as he walked down by the lake and picked up a stone and tried to skip it across the water. It didn't go far. He picked up another stone. His mind flashed back to earlier. "Did I do okay back there?"

"Yeah, ya did great, lad," replied the little gnome enthusiastically.

Digger thought for a moment.

"So what do you believe, Patrick O'Toole?" he asked.

"Me?" responded Patrick.

"Yeah, you," confirmed Digger. "What do you believe, Patrick O'Toole?"

"Well, lad, I'm a simple sort of fella," confided the gnome. "Mainly, I just believe what I've experienced, what I understand, and what I see. Always concluded that I was born with a brain and me senses for a reason. Don't ya think?"

"I guess so," smiled Digger. How refreshing, he thought. Everybody could use a little of that attitude. His grandfather was right. It was easy to be fond of Patrick O'Toole.

The young lad turned and gallivanted down to the edge of the lake and sent his flat slate stone skipping across the water.

What a throw! The stone bounced six or seven times across the surface of the lake.

"Did you see that?" exclaimed Digger.

But Patrick O'Toole didn't respond. When Digger turned to look, he discovered the stone supporting only the emerald charm. The little gnome had vanished. In the distance, Digger heard the church bells beginning to chime. Six o'clock! His day in the Orchard was over. Digger grabbed the charm and ran quickly to the tree and climbed inside to wish farewell to Patrick O'Toole. But when he stood up this time, he drove his head hard into solid wood.

The pain was excruciating. Digger slumped to the ground inside the tree. Everything went dark. His skull throbbed. He clutched his head to ease the pain.

A few seconds later, Digger felt a firm round object poke him in the ribs.

"Don't," pleaded Digger.

The round object poked him once again. Digger opened his eyes and realized that he was actually sitting at the base of the orchard's stone wall. Even more shocking, he found himself staring into the eyes of the orchard's owner, Michael O'Toole, who had obviously been poking Digger with his walking stick.

"Sir, I . . . I . . . ," stuttered Digger grasping for an excuse.

Surprisingly, Michael O'Toole's expression, though stern, hinted of curiosity more than anger. The proprietor motioned with his stick for Digger to get over the wall and out of his orchard immediately.

Digger scrambled to his feet and began to climb over the wall. An unexpected boost from Michael O'Toole helped Digger over his obstacle in a controlled manner.

"Better get, boy, before those dogs come back," he snapped.

Digger dropped to the ground on the other side of the wall and hurried over to the wrought iron fence and latched onto the horizontal bar. As he slipped through the slender opening, he heard Michael O'Toole chuckle as if he were amused.

Digger dropped down onto the sidewalk and began to hurry home.

"Did that really happen?" he wondered.

THE END

Chandler McEwan was born in Connecticut in 1950 and moved with his family to Kentucky seven years later. Chandler graduated from the University of Kentucky in 1974 and is married with two children.

Although O'Toole's Orchard is obviously a light-hearted fantasy intended to entertain and be gently thought provoking, the story does reflect the author's very real struggle as a youth to resolve the conflicting ideologies of Christianity and Evolution. The outlook on life shared by the gnome near the end of the story represents a point of view also embraced by the writer.

CHANDLERMC@aol.com

www.ingramcontent.com/pod-product-compliance
Lightning Source LLC
Chambersburg PA
CBHW070529130626
46555CB00003B/1334